Nobody Cares About Me!

For Lucy and Jonathan – AR

For M & D – AK

First Published in Great Britain in 1997
Bloomsbury Publishing Plc, 38 Soho Square, London W1V 5DF

Copyright © Text Alison Ritchie 1997
Copyright © Illustrations Ann Kronheimer 1997
Art Direction Lisa Coombes

The moral right of the author and illustrator has been asserted
A CIP catalogue record of this book is available from the
British Library

ISBN 0 7475 3051 3

Printed by Bath Press, Great Britain

10 9 8 7 6 5 4 3 2 1

Little Readers

Nobody Cares About Me!

Alison Ritchie

Pictures by Ann Kronheimer

Bloomsbury Children's Books

My name is Casey.

This is my mum.

This is my dad.

This is my fish (called Fish).

And this is my sad story.

Once upon a time,
when I was one,
Mum used to say
I was her little heart-throb.

Dad used to say I was his little cherub.

Fish loved me too.

When I was two,
Mum used to say I
was the bee's knees.

Dad used to say I
was the cat's whiskers.

Fish used to say
glug glug.

When I was three,
Mum used to say,
"What would I do without you?"

Dad used to say, "You're my pride and joy."

Fish used to say
glug glug.

When I was four,
Mum used to give
me sloppy kisses.

Dad used to give
me high fives.

Fish used to let me tickle his back.

Then when I was five . . .

HE turned up.
This is HIM.

Now HE'S Mum's little heart-throb

and Dad's little cherub.

And nobody cares about me!
Not even Fish.

What's so special about
HIM I want to know.

How come he gets to
stay up after I'm in bed?

How come he gets milk
whenever he wants it?

How come he gets pushed
around and I have to walk?

Nobody cares about ME!

When HE does something naughty, everyone laughs.
When I do something naughty, I get told off.

When HE talks, "Gaa gaa gaa,"
everyone says, "Clever boy!"
When I talk, everyone says, "Be quiet, Casey."

When HE throws a ball, everyone claps
and says, "Clever boy."
When I throw a ball, it's,
"Behave yourself, Casey!"

When HE bangs
his drum, everyone
cheers. When I bang
my drum, everyone tut-tuts,
"What a horrible noise, Casey."

Nobody cares about ME!

Well I don't care about THEM, either.

Today we went to the zoo, Mum, Dad, me and HIM.
I was in a grump. (You can't blame me, can you?)
HE was in a grump.
Me and Him. Grump, grump, grump.

HE was in a worse grump than me, though.

He threw his ice cream at Mum.
He wiped his hands on Dad's trousers.
Then he screamed at the top of his voice.

That was funny.

Then he made a
rude noise.

That was even funnier.

Mum and Dad got cross – with HIM!!
(and not with ME!!)

So he did it again!
I laughed, then he laughed.

Mum and Dad got FURIOUS!!

My baby brother was definitely
in their BAD BOOKS!

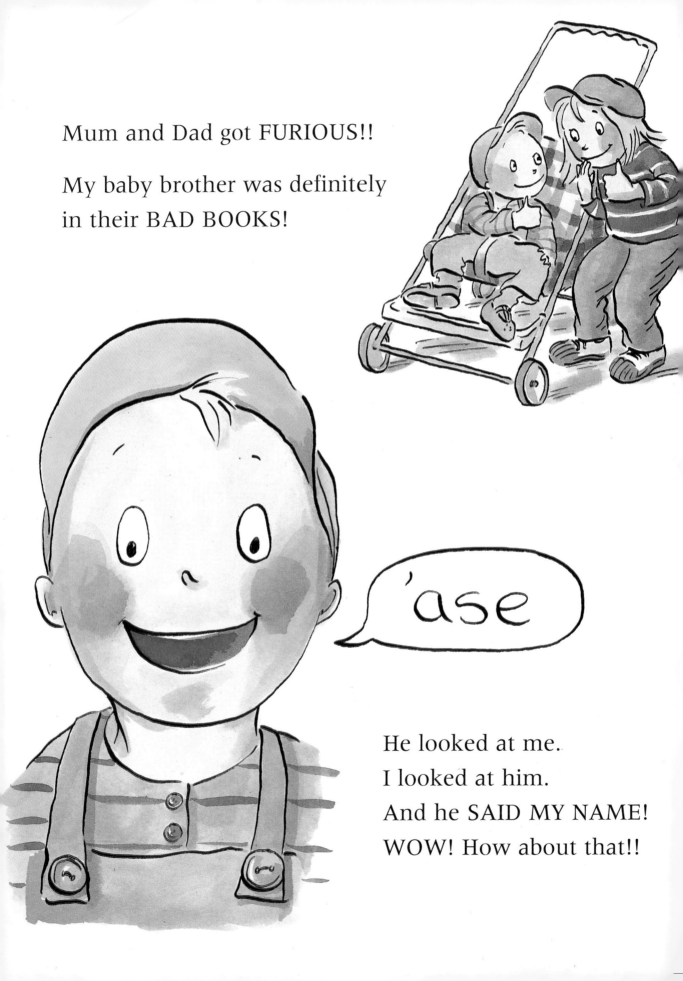

'ase

He looked at me.
I looked at him.
And he SAID MY NAME!
WOW! How about that!!

I pushed him round the zoo all day.
When he chucked his cup down, I picked it up.
When he threw his hat away, I ran to get it.
When he took his shoes off, I put them back on.

He was so naughty, and I was so good,
Mum and Dad think I'm a hero.

"My little heart-throb, you're the bee's knees, what would I do without you?" said Mum.

"My little cherub, you're the cat's whiskers, you're my pride and joy," said Dad.

And HE said my name (again!) and smiled at me.
He really likes me!
(By the way, he's called Max.)

Now I never say, "Nobody cares about me."

Well, hardly ever.